The HIV/AIDS Pandemic

John Allen

San Diego, CA

About the Author

John Allen is a writer who lives in Oklahoma City.

© 2022 ReferencePoint Press, Inc.
Printed in the United States

For more information, contact:
ReferencePoint Press, Inc.
PO Box 27779
San Diego, CA 92198
www.ReferencePointPress.com

LIBRARY OF CONGRESS CATALOGING-IN-PUBLICATION DATA

Names: Allen, John, 1957- author.
Title: The HIV/AIDS pandemic / by John Allen.
Description: San Diego, CA : ReferencePoint Press, 2022. | Series: Historic
    pandemics and plagues | Includes bibliographical references and index.
Identifiers: LCCN 2020057721 (print) | LCCN 2020057722 (ebook) | ISBN
    9781678201029 (library binding) | ISBN 9781678201036 (ebook)
Subjects: LCSH: AIDS (Disease)--Juvenile literature.
Classification: LCC RA643.8 A46 2022 (print) | LCC RA643.8 (ebook) | DDC
    614.5/99392--dc23
LC record available at https://lccn.loc.gov/2020057721
LC ebook record available at https://lccn.loc.gov/2020057722

CONTENTS

Important Events During the HIV/AIDS Pandemic

1983
French researchers at the Pasteur Institute in Paris isolate the virus HIV-1.

1984
Ryan White, a thirteen-year-old in Indiana who suffers from hemophilia, contracts HIV from a contaminated blood transfusion.

1981
The first cases of AIDS are detected among gay men in Southern California. Michael Gottlieb, a doctor at UCLA, writes the first report about the disease for the CDC.

1989
ACT UP protesters disrupt a service at New York City's St. Patrick's Cathedral to oppose Archbishop John O'Connor's anti-condom message.

1980	1982	1984	1986	1988

1982
The CDC adopts the name acquired immune deficiency syndrome, or AIDS, for the disease.

1985
Robert Gallo of the National Cancer Institute wins approval for an enzyme-based blood test for HIV antibodies.

1988
The WHO announces World AIDS Day on December 1, which is still observed today.

1987
The FDA approves the antiretroviral drug AZT as the first treatment for AIDS.

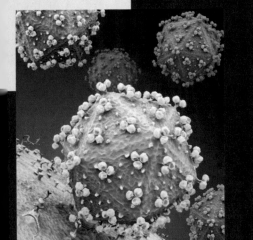

1998
A street protest and petition drive in Cape Town, South Africa, lead to the formation of the Treatment Action Campaign, one of the world's most effective AIDS activist groups.

2003
The Bush administration creates the President's Emergency Plan for AIDS Relief. It later becomes a key component of the Obama administration's Global Health Initiative.

1994
AIDS becomes the leading cause of death for Americans 25 to 44 years of age.

2005
The WHO, UNAIDS, and the Global Fund to Fight AIDS, Tuberculosis and Malaria join together to increase availability of antiretroviral drugs in developing nations.

1990
ACT UP wins a court battle in New York City to promote needle exchange for IV drug users susceptible to HIV.

2010
The Obama administration lifts the long-standing ban on travel and immigration for people who are HIV positive.

2012
The FDA approves OraQuick, the first in-home test for HIV.

1990	2000	2010	2020	2030

1991
Los Angeles Lakers basketball star Earvin "Magic" Johnson retires after testing positive for HIV.

1997
Highly active antiretroviral therapy reduces AIDS-related deaths by more than 40 percent compared to the previous year.

2020
According to a December CDC report, the rate of HIV-related deaths in the United States fell by nearly half from 2010 to 2017.

2019
The Trump administration launches a drive to distribute HIV-prevention drugs such as Truvada free to people who lack prescription drug insurance coverage.

5

An Ongoing Battle Against HIV

Sibongile Zulu, a single mother of four living in South Africa, was trying not to panic. In August 2020 she had no idea how she would get the HIV medications she desperately needed. She had been laid off from her office job in the COVID-19 lockdown. Now the government-run clinic had run out of her HIV drugs, and she lacked the forty-eight dollars needed to buy them at the local pharmacy. Being HIV positive, Zulu has a damaged immune system, which makes her more susceptible to infections, including from the novel coronavirus. Eventually, she managed to obtain the lifesaving drugs from a local charity. But a study by the United Nations warns that others may not be so fortunate. Disruptions in supplies of anti-HIV medications could result in an additional five hundred thousand AIDS-related deaths in sub-Saharan Africa. Although great strides have been made in HIV treatments, those infected still face large challenges from day to day. Health experts urge that these people not be forgotten. "The COVID-19 pandemic must not be an excuse to divert investment from HIV," says Winnie Byanyima, executive director of the Joint United Nations Programme on HIV/AIDS (UNAIDS). "There is a risk that the hard-earned gains of the AIDS response will be sacrificed to the fight against COVID-19, but the right to health means that no one disease should be fought at the expense of the other."[1]

A Worldwide Scourge

Zulu is one of millions around the world infected with HIV, or human immunodeficiency virus. The virus attacks a person's immune system, reducing its ability to fight off infections and other diseases. If not controlled with medications, HIV can lead to AIDS, an advanced condition that often is fatal. AIDS stands for acquired immune deficiency syndrome. Each year hundreds of thousands of people die from HIV/AIDS globally, making it one of the world's most deadly infectious diseases. In 2019 South Africa reported the highest number of AIDS-related deaths for any nation, with more than seventy-two thousand victims. About 38 million people in the world currently live with HIV. In the United States about 1.2 million people have the virus. According to the Centers for Disease Control and Prevention (CDC), in 2018 (the most recent year for which data are available) there were almost sixteen thousand deaths among those diagnosed with HIV in the United States. For Americans aged twenty-five to forty-four, HIV/AIDS is the sixth-most frequent cause of death.

"There is a risk that the hard-earned gains of the AIDS response will be sacrificed to the fight against COVID-19, but the right to health means that no one disease should be fought at the expense of the other."[1]

—Winnie Byanyima, executive director of UNAIDS

HIV is transmitted through exchange of bodily fluids such as blood and semen. This means a person can be infected through shared needles, blood transfusions, and unprotected sex with a male or female. A mother can pass the virus to her unborn child. Unlike COVID-19 and similar viruses, HIV is not spread by coughing, sneezing, or spitting or through casual contact such as a hug or handshake. Health officials have stressed the fact that people with HIV pose no threat to others through normal social interactions. Officials do recommend that those who are sexually active get tested, even if they use protection. Discovering the virus early is crucial to effective treatment.

Once infected with HIV, a person has it for life. The virus kills off a certain kind of T cell necessary for the body's defense against infections and cancers. If not controlled, the infection can progress into full-blown AIDS and a breakdown of the immune system. Victims in the late stages of AIDS can look skeletal, with skin lesions all over their bodies. However, due to advances in drugs for treatment, HIV infection is no longer a death sentence. Beginning in the late 1980s, breakthroughs in research brought treatments that could control HIV and prevent the onset of AIDS. HIV-positive individuals like Zulu can now live normal lives for decades with the virus.

Crisis and Controversy

HIV/AIDS first came to public attention in the United States in the early 1980s. Since its first victims were gay men in large coastal cities, it was often labeled a gay disease. The virus became prey to politics and controversy. Some critics, including conservative religious leaders and politicians, blamed the victims. They insisted that AIDS was spread by reckless behaviors involving sex and drugs. However, gay activists fought back. Seeing their friends dying in large numbers, they worked to dispel false beliefs about the disease and how it was transmitted. They urged that no stigma be attached to AIDS sufferers. They organized huge rallies for AIDS research and lobbied federal health agencies to slice through red tape in order to find a cure. The battle against HIV/AIDS ended up energizing the movement for gay rights in America. "We didn't have a gay center then or much in the way of gay organizations," says Jesse Peel, an Atlanta psychiatrist and gay community organizer. "As the epidemic unfolded, it began to bring people together."[2]

"Today, with the right tools, right data, and right leadership, we must seize the historic opportunity to control and ultimately end the HIV epidemic, community by community."[3]

—Deborah L. Birx, US global AIDS coordinator, and Brett P. Giroir, assistant secretary of health

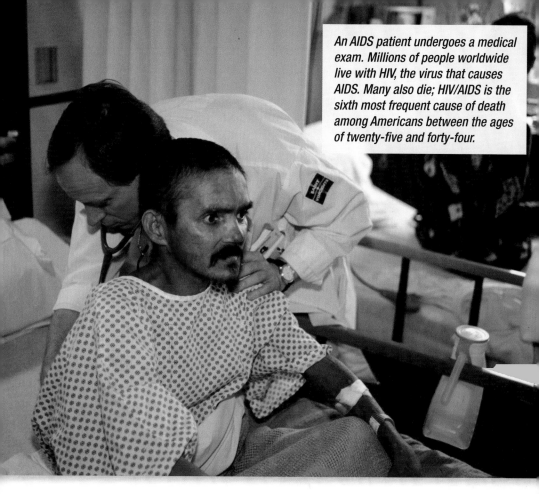

An AIDS patient undergoes a medical exam. Millions of people worldwide live with HIV, the virus that causes AIDS. Many also die; HIV/AIDS is the sixth most frequent cause of death among Americans between the ages of twenty-five and forty-four.

In the United States, Europe, sub-Saharan Africa, and other centers of the outbreak, HIV/AIDS has affected a wide range of people. Victims have included men and women, gay and straight people, young and old, rural dwellers and urbanites. Diagnosing and treating HIV/AIDS patients remains a health priority around the world. According to Deborah L. Birx, US global AIDS coordinator, and Brett P. Giroir, assistant secretary of health, "Today, with the right tools, right data, and right leadership, we must seize the historic opportunity to control and ultimately end the HIV epidemic, community by community."[3]

CHAPTER ONE

The Origins of HIV

For Michael Gottlieb, the reports were puzzling but impossible to ignore. Gottlieb, a thirty-three-year-old assistant professor at the University of California, Los Angeles (UCLA), Medical Center, had been looking for a patient with an immune system illness that he could discuss with his students. In one emergency ward, Gottlieb met a young gay man who complained of fevers, sudden weight loss, and a weakened immune system. His white blood cell count was dangerously low, and his mouth and throat were raw with a fungal infection. "Well, we scratched our heads as to what he might have," recalls Gottlieb. "It was just such a striking, dramatic illness, and he was so critically ill. It was a distinctly unusual thing for someone previously healthy to walk into a hospital so significantly ill. It just didn't fit any recognized disease or syndrome that we were aware of."[4]

A Mysterious New Disease

Soon Gottlieb learned that several gay men in Southern California were showing similar symptoms. Curiosity led him to investigate. A Los Angeles physician named Joel Weisman was treating two gay patients who also had unexplained fevers, as well as swollen lymph nodes and intestinal illness. A fourth patient in Santa Monica had shown the same signs before dying of pneumonia. A fifth young patient in Beverly Hills not only had a lung infection but also Kaposi's sarcoma, a rare skin cancer sometimes seen in older people with damaged immune systems. Tests showed that the patients, along with several more referrals, were all deficient in CD4, a certain type of T cell needed for healthy immune response. Connecting the evidence, Gottlieb believed that he had possibly discovered a mysterious new disease.

A colleague advised him to summarize his findings in an article for the CDC. Gottlieb's brief article, published in the CDC's *Morbidity and Mortality Weekly Report* on June 5, 1981, drew little attention at first. However, his discovery would soon sweep through the medical community. It would also raise alarms across the United States and eventually the world. Gottlieb's report was the first description of AIDS on record.

A month after Gottlieb's CDC article appeared, the *New York Times* published its first story on HIV/AIDS. On July 3, 1981, a doctor and medical correspondent named Lawrence K. Altman described the outbreak of a rare cancer among gay men. Altman explained that the cancer, called Kaposi's sarcoma, emerged first as violet spots on the skin. It often caused swollen lymph glands and rapidly turned deadly by spreading throughout the body. The patients' immune systems were shown to have severe defects. Altman also noted that doctors were stymied about the origins of the disease. "The cause of the outbreak is unknown," Altman wrote, "and there is as yet no evidence of contagion. But the doctors who have made the diagnoses, mostly in New York City and the San Francisco Bay area, are alerting other physicians who treat large numbers of homosexual men to the problem in an effort to help identify more cases and to reduce the delay in offering chemotherapy treatment."[5] The article quoted a CDC spokesperson who said no cases had been reported outside the gay community or in women.

> "The doctors who have made the diagnoses . . . are alerting other physicians who treat large numbers of homosexual men to the problem in an effort to help identify more cases and to reduce the delay in offering chemotherapy treatment."[5]
>
> —Lawrence K. Altman, a medical journalist for the *New York Times*

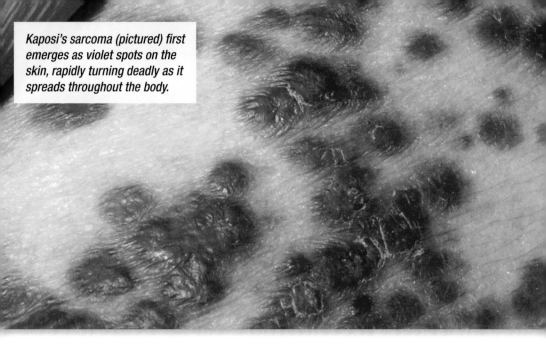

Kaposi's sarcoma (pictured) first emerges as violet spots on the skin, rapidly turning deadly as it spreads throughout the body.

Altman would go on to be one of the foremost chroniclers of the AIDS pandemic. Following his report in the *New York Times*, stories quickly appeared in news outlets such as the Associated Press, National Public Radio, CNN, and the *Washington Post*. By the end of 1981, 270 cases of severe immune deficiency had been reported among gay men in America, with 121 deaths. Some news outlets began referring to the as yet unnamed disease as a gay cancer. Yet cases of pneumocystis pneumonia, a rare lung infection associated with the disease, were also found in people who injected drugs. There was still much to be learned about the mysterious illness.

Not Confined to Gay Men

Gottlieb continued to lead the way in research on the new disease. In December 1981 he joined with Weisman and five other colleagues to publish a paper in the prestigious *New England Journal of Medicine*. The authors described the disease as an immune deficiency that likely could be passed from person to person. They noted that patients tended to have random infections, pneumocystis pneumonia, and Kaposi's sarcoma, all conditions associated with a weakened immune system. Several patients also had a virus that infects DNA called cytomegalovirus (CMV). The authors were not sure whether the CMV was the cause of the immune deficiency or the result of it. They also proposed that the disease might be caused by a sexually transmitted agent, such as a virus. Gottlieb and his colleagues would prove to be mostly accurate in their guesses about the illness and its causes. As for Gottlieb himself, his place in medical history was assured. He had accomplished his ambition to discover, describe, and help treat a potentially deadly new disease. He would forever be associated with HIV/AIDS, one of the most controversial diseases—both medically and politically—of the twentieth century.

Descriptions of the new disease in the *New England Journal of Medicine* reached far more physicians and immunology experts than the earlier CDC piece had. It set off shock waves in the medical world. A rush to gather more information about the disease helped puncture certain early myths. For example, the disease was definitively not confined to gay men. Cases were found among heterosexual men and women, immigrants from Haiti and other nations, intravenous (IV) drug users, hemophiliacs, and even infants. Evidence mounted that the disease was passed along through exchange of bodily fluids such as blood, semen, vaginal secretions, and breast milk. It could be contracted by having sex, sharing needles for drug use, or getting a blood transfusion. It seemed to be related to other viral infections such as CMV, hepatitis B, and herpes, which were found in many of the patients.

Knowledge about the disease helped experts avoid misnaming it. Initially, it was called gay-related immune deficiency, or GRID. However, by September 1982 medical experts had settled on the name acquired immune deficiency syndrome, or AIDS. This emphasized that anyone could get the disease. Nonetheless, social stigma related to AIDS began to grow. Jokes arose about AIDS victims as the so-called 4-H Club: homosexuals, hemophiliacs, heroin users, and Haitians.

Discovering HIV

Scientists the world over were searching for what caused AIDS. Some scientists began to examine a family of viruses called retroviruses. A retrovirus replicates itself, or spreads, by inserting a reverse-coded copy of its genes into the DNA of a host cell. In 1983 a team of young French researchers at the Pasteur Institute in Paris found the culprit among the retroviruses they were studying. They isolated it from a culture in the swollen lymph nodes of an AIDS-infected gay man. The team, led by Françoise Barré-Sinoussi, called the virus lymphadenopathy-associated virus. The deadly virus would later be identified as HIV-1. The medical community hailed the speed of the discovery, coming just two years after AIDS had emerged in the United States. In 2008 Barré-Sinoussi and her boss at the institute, Luc Montagnier, would share the Nobel Prize for the discovery. In truth, Barré-Sinoussi and her team deserved the main credit. As Robert Bazell reported for NBC News, "[Montagnier] knew little of retroviruses, and Barré-Sinoussi and her colleagues had to spend many afternoons explaining to him what a retrovirus was and why they believed one to be the cause of the new disease."[6]

The discovery of HIV also led to a diagnostic blood test for the virus. On March 2, 1985, Robert Gallo, a lead researcher at the National Cancer Institute at Bethesda, Maryland, won approval for the enzyme-based ELISA blood test for antibodies linked to HIV infection. Gallo claimed to have discovered HIV before Montagnier's French team, although he used cultures borrowed from the Pasteur Institute in his own research. The cultures helped Gallo develop an HIV test with great speed. Health officials viewed the new blood test for HIV as a medical necessity—not to protect individuals but to secure the blood supply. Reports about patients receiving blood transfusions tainted with HIV threatened to set off a panic in the United States. More than 140 Americans had already contracted HIV from transfusions. The first tests of blood donations were very sensitive in order to catch any viral traces. As a result, they showed a high rate of false positives, although the overall rate of positives was low. The new test eased fears by ensuring that

The Myth of Patient Zero

The early years of the AIDS crisis saw many stories and rumors that were later shown to be false. One of the most persistent tales was the myth of the so-called Patient Zero. In 1982 the CDC interviewed several gay men suffering from AIDS in Los Angeles. The investigators hoped to trace sexual contacts to determine the path of infection. One person kept appearing: a gay French Canadian flight attendant named Gaétan Dugas. Allegedly, Dugas, who died of AIDS in 1984, had had sexual contacts not only on the West Coast but in New York City and other North American cities. In his 1987 book on the AIDS crisis, *And the Band Played On*, author Randy Shilts referred to Dugas as Patient Zero, the ultimate source of the US epidemic.

Later research demolished this narrative. In 2016 a genetic analysis of Dugas's blood sample showed that he could not have been a base case for the HIV strains in the early 1980s. According to Richard McKay, a medical historian at the University of Cambridge in England, "The historical evidence has been pointing to the fallacy of Patient Zero for decades. We now have additional phylogenetic evidence that helps to consolidate this position."

Quoted in Science Daily, "AIDS: The Making of the 'Patient Zero' Myth," October 26, 2016. www.sciencedaily.com.

all donated blood would be screened for HIV. By August 1, 1985, America's blood supply was declared HIV-free.

Gallo's test also enabled people to find out if they had HIV. Getting the test could be fraught with anxiety, since the disease had no known cure or effective treatment. Moreover, potential discrimination against HIV-positive individuals led to fears about testing altogether. Some people declined even to be seen getting tested. The first ELISA test kits featured the following label: "It is inappropriate to use this test as a screen for AIDS or as a screen for members of groups at increased risk for AIDS in the general population. The presence of [the HIV] antibody is NOT a diagnosis of AIDS."[7] There were also special protocols added for individual tests, such as retesting positive results. In March 1986 the CDC recommended that people in so-called high-risk groups—including gay people and IV drug users—get periodic tests for the virus. The question of how HIV testing should be used would lead to controversy going forward.

The Virus Goes Global

Scientists also addressed another basic question about HIV/ AIDS: Where did it originate? Research traced the virus's beginnings to the Democratic Republic of the Congo in the early 1920s. The blood-borne and sexually transmitted disease spread slowly until it reached larger population centers. In the mid-1960s the virus apparently moved from the African nation of Zaire to Haiti in the Western Hemisphere. Scientists found evidence of HIV infection in the United States as early as 1971, a decade before it was widely reported. By 1983, HIV/AIDS had also spread to fifteen European countries, seven Latin American countries, Canada, Zaire, Haiti, Australia, and Japan.

Cases in Europe emerged around two groups: gay men who had visited the United States or people with ties to Central Africa. Among the first AIDS victims in Europe were two Spanish hemophiliacs who had received tainted blood transfusions while in America. The disease seemed to spread less rapidly in Europe

AIDS patients weigh themselves at a hospital in Haiti. By 1983 HIV/AIDS had spread to Haiti and to many countries in Europe, Latin America, and elsewhere.

than in the United States. Health experts theorize that this was due to less clustering of gay people and drug users in large European cities. However, by the mid-1980s, Europe was forced to confront its own AIDS crisis. Faced with a rising number of HIV diagnoses, European health officials joined with the World Health Organization to declare the disease an epidemic. By the end of the decade, every region on earth had reported cases.

Fears about the outbreak disrupted international travel. In 1987 the United States banned all HIV-positive people from getting US tourist visas or permanent residence status without a special waiver. To critics, the ban was unnecessary and merely showed the stigma attached to the disease. Undertaken at the height of AIDS panic, this policy denied access to many performers and artists, not to mention ordinary visitors with friends or relatives in America. When President Barack Obama ended the ban in 2010, American health experts rejoiced. "I think there's reason to be joyful that the ban has been lifted because a ban like this sends the message that somehow we're going to protect ourselves from HIV by not letting people with HIV come into the country," said Tom Coates, a global health expert at UCLA. "And the truth of the matter is that's not how we protect ourselves from HIV."[8]

Attacking the Body

As the virus drew more public notice, people were shocked to see its effects on victims. Those with full-blown AIDS looked like walking skeletons, often too weak to care for themselves. HIV attacks a person's body by targeting the immune system. It damages vital cells called CD4 T cells, rendering the body progressively less able to fight off other infections. Once the immune system is wrecked, typically mild infections, called opportunistic infections, become dangerous. For a person with advanced AIDS, the environment teems with life-threatening pathogens for which they have no defense.

The disease unfolds in stages. The first stage is called primary or acute HIV infection. A person who contracts HIV may develop flu-like symptoms within one month. The symptoms may persist for several days or weeks. They include fever and chills, sore throat, joint or muscle pain, swollen glands, mouth ulcers, night sweats, and fatigue. Some people do not experience any symptoms. Physicians refer to this stage as seroconversion illness. During this period, the person's immune system is fighting the infection by producing antibodies against it. Those without symptoms may be unaware that they have HIV. That is why regular testing is vital.

The second stage, called chronic infection, can last for ten years or more. Some people experience no symptoms or very mild ones. Yet if left untreated, HIV can continue to multiply in the body. This causes a person to advance to the third and final stage, which is full-blown AIDS. A person who is HIV positive is considered to have AIDS when his or her CD4 cells have been reduced to fewer than two hundred per cubic millimeter of blood. AIDS is also diagnosed when the person begins to get cancers and opportunistic infections such as lung infections. These ailments, which generally would be resisted by people with strong immune systems, are more frequent and more severe for patients with AIDS. They may include Kaposi's sarcoma, a cancer that appears as bruise-like skin lesions and attacks the lungs, intestines, or lymph nodes; CMV, which invades the brain, lungs, and belly; lymphoma, which is cancer of the lymph nodes; tuberculosis, which is a bacterial lung infection; and salmonella septicemia, which overwhelms the immune system with bacteria. AIDS can also damage a person's eyes, heart, kidneys, and digestive system. It weakens the bones, leaving them brittle and more apt to break. Inflammation of the brain and spinal cord can cause confusion, memory loss, lack of balance, and seizures. Most people who die from AIDS do not die from the disease itself but from these related infections.

HIV Wasting Syndrome

In the final stage of AIDS, a patient may seem to waste away. This means not just loss of fat but also loss of lean muscle mass. Infections force the body to burn 10 percent more calories than normal.

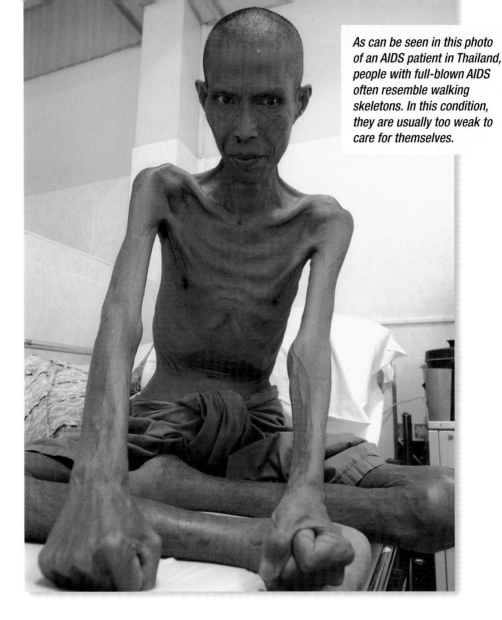

As can be seen in this photo of an AIDS patient in Thailand, people with full-blown AIDS often resemble walking skeletons. In this condition, they are usually too weak to care for themselves.

Also, the body has reduced ability to absorb nutrients. Due to constant stress, a patient's cells grow inflamed, and the body begins to attack its own fat tissue, protein, and muscle mass. The result is that patients have a shrunken, skeletal appearance, with hollow eyes, protruding bones, and a severe lack of energy. In 1987 the CDC classified this as HIV wasting syndrome and called it an AIDS-defining condition—which at that point meant almost certain death. It would be years before medical science developed effective treatments allowing people with HIV to survive the disease.

Jonathan Grimshaw, an HIV survivor and activist in the United Kingdom who contracted the disease in 1984, recalls the sight of so many friends wasting away and dying. He says:

> It's so horrific looking back. I don't look back very often. It's hard to conceive that it was actually happening—you'd get phonecalls to say, "So and so is ill," and it wasn't that they were ill—they were dying. And you would see them dying. Over the course of a couple of years, you would see them wasting away, you'd go to see them in hospital and you'd go to their funerals. And it was one after another. I don't know how we did it.[9]

An Urgent Search for Treatments

Emerging in the early 1980s, HIV/AIDS swiftly grew into a worldwide health crisis. The early research of doctors like Michael Gottlieb identified the symptoms of the new disease and pro-

A Sadly Typical Story

In the early 1980s, harrowing accounts of AIDS victims brought home to the public how the disease ravaged its victims. Deotis McMather's story was sadly typical. McMather left his native Virginia to live in San Francisco's Tenderloin district, one of the epicenters of the outbreak. He sold sex for money and injected drugs with the proceeds. In April 1982 McMather began to notice purple blotches all over his body. His body had stopped producing platelets to clot his blood, so each bump or bruise would continue leaking blood under the skin. In the fall McMather checked into San Francisco General Hospital for tests. He never left.

McMather's loss of platelets caused his abdominal organs to become inflamed. Doctors removed his spleen and part of his stomach and liver. The operation left a lurid stapled gash across his bloated stomach. "His condition deteriorated when his lungs started filling with fluid," wrote AIDS chronicler Randy Shilts. "He was put on a respirator, but after a few days, he asked to be taken off the machine. Within an hour, twenty-seven-year-old Deotis McMather was dead."

Randy Shilts, *And the Band Played On: Politics, People, and the AIDS Epidemic.* New York: St. Martin's Griffin, 2007.

vided warnings to people most at risk. Attempts to classify AIDS as strictly a gay disease gave way to facts showing that anyone, regardless if sexual orientation, could be infected. French researchers succeeded in isolating HIV, leading to the development of antibody tests for the virus. By the end of the 1980s, doctors and medical experts were still scrambling to find treatments. As *Time* magazine's Claudia Wallis noted, "It is the virtual certainty of death from AIDS, once the syndrome has fully developed, that makes the disease so frightening, along with the uncertainty of nearly everything else about it."[10]

"It is the virtual certainty of death from AIDS, once the syndrome has fully developed, that makes the disease so frightening."[10]

—Claudia Wallis, a reporter for *Time* magazine

CHAPTER TWO

Solidarity and Stigma

On Sunday morning, December 10, 1989, a massive crowd of AIDS activists gathered outside New York City's St. Patrick's Cathedral. The protesters were venting their anger at Cardinal Archbishop John O'Connor's opposition to the use of condoms—a practice health experts deemed vital to reducing the dangerous spread of AIDS. For the protesters, O'Connor's stance posed a real threat to the gay community. As the 10:15 morning mass approached, dozens of the activists filed into the cathedral along with the regular parishioners. Their plan was to express their outrage without disrespecting other churchgoers. They would interrupt O'Connor's sermon by standing as a group while one of them read a statement, then turn their backs on the archbishop in protest.

However, some of the protesters declined to follow the script. Michael Petrelis stood up on a pew and began to blow an ear-piercing whistle. Then Petrelis yelled, "Stop killing us! Archbishop O'Connor, stop killing us!"[11] Suddenly, several protesters joined Petrelis's chant, while others fell to the floor as if they were dying and then refused to move. Police arrived to drag the demonstrators out of the sanctuary. When O'Connor resumed the service, one protester joined the line to receive communion. Instead of accepting the communion wafer, the young man crumbled it onto the floor—a sacrilege in the Catholic faith. News reports about the incident sparked outrage about the protesters' tactics. Many fellow activists agreed that the disturbance had gone too far. But a core group of supporters viewed the protests as a righteous display. As Petrelis admitted later, "I felt there was just not enough anger that could be heard."[12]

An Urgent Political Cause

From the earliest days of the outbreak, AIDS became an urgent political cause in the gay community. Many gay individuals feared the disease would reverse the gains they had made in equal rights and social acceptance since the 1960s. Events like the Stonewall uprising in June 1969, in which gay people in New York's Greenwich Village had rioted against a police raid on the Stonewall Inn, a popular gay bar, had built a new solidarity among gay men, lesbians, and bisexuals. People who had once been closeted came out to march in gay pride parades and support political groups like the Gay Liberation Front. But the social stigma of AIDS threatened to derail such progress.

Soon after the first news stories about the disease appeared, conservative voices rang out to deplore what they called the gay lifestyle. They pointed to a doctor's claim in the *New York Times* that gay men with the disease had had sex with many different partners—as many as ten a night up to four times a week. Some critics blamed the outbreak exclusively on reckless sex practices and drug use. Right-wing political columnist Pat Buchanan declared that AIDS was nature's revenge on homosexuals and showed that gay people were not only a physical menace but a moral menace to America. Critics like Buchanan took advantage of the overall lack of knowledge about the disease to spread false information and feed the public's fears. They raised alarms about gay people working in bars, restaurants, or any job that involved food handling. They urged landlords to evict tenants suspected of having the disease.

Such fearmongering led to widespread panic. Many people shunned any physical contact with AIDS victims and dreaded even being in the same room with them. These fears extended to nurses and medical workers who refused to treat AIDS patients. Cliff Morrison, who worked as a nurse at San Francisco General Hospital in 1983, recalls his shock and disgust at how AIDS patients were being neglected by the staff. Some were left lying in their own urine and excrement. Used food trays piled up in their rooms. "I would go in patients' rooms and you could tell that they hadn't had a bath," Morrison says. "They weren't being taken care of."[13] To remedy the situation, Morrison joined with other health care workers to create Ward 5B, an inpatient special care unit for AIDS victims at San Francisco General Hospital. Morrison and his team strove to treat each patient with dignity and respect. They encouraged family members to visit and allowed the patients to have pets. They made a point of touching their patients casually as they tended to their needs and offered comfort. Morrison says:

"I would go in [AIDS] patients' rooms and you could tell that they hadn't had a bath. They weren't being taken care of."[13]

—Cliff Morrison, a nurse at San Francisco General Hospital

What I was hearing from the specialists around us with the information that was coming out, was that I wasn't at risk providing care to people by touching people. And everybody around us was saying, "Oh you're just being cavalier. This is really not what you should be doing, and you're giving the wrong message." And our response always was, "We're giving the right message." So we were dealing with a lot of hysteria and misinformation and just outright discrimination, I think, very early on.[14]

In those early years of the pandemic, with no effective treatments available, Morrison and his team could not prevent their patients from dying. However, they could give them a homelike environment and treat them with compassion. Morrison's ideas for Ward 5B would influence humane AIDS care nationwide.

Providing Services for HIV Victims

Members of the gay community also saw the need for accurate information and specialized care. In August 1981 Larry Kramer, a gay screenwriter and novelist, hosted a meeting of eighty prominent gay individuals to address the growing crisis. The meeting included doctors, attorneys, writers, and artists. They commiserated over mutual friends who had been laid low by AIDS with such shocking speed. They traded stories of AIDS patients suffering neglect from frightened health care workers and funeral parlors refusing to handle services for AIDS victims. Kramer noted that the hysterical tone of recent news reports about the disease had him worried that a backlash against gay people was building. Outspoken and cantankerous, he stressed the need to fight for the gay community. As a group, they could advocate for AIDS research and ease the growing feelings of helplessness and fear with a message of hope. In his apartment that day, Kramer, novelist Edmund White, and the rest of the guests chipped in a total of $7,000 to fund their efforts. On January 4, 1982, they launched the Gay Men's Health Crisis (GMHC), the first nonprofit AIDS service organization in the world. The GMHC pledged to fight the disease and provide support for all those affected.

The group's first act was to set up a twenty-four-hour hotline to provide up-to-date information about HIV/AIDS and dispel rumors and falsehoods. It began as the answering machine in a volunteer's apartment. One hundred calls came in the first night. Certain questions required advice from medical and legal experts. The GMHC set up a patient services division to direct callers to get help. In 1983 the CDC acknowledged the hotline's success by establishing its own version for AIDS patients around the country.

Soon the GMHC was opening an office on West Twenty-Second Street in New York and distributing fifty thousand free copies of its AIDS newsletter to doctors, clinics, hospitals, and the Library of Congress. It began a hugely successful Buddy program, in which volunteers—male and female, gay and straight—helped people with AIDS attend to their day-to-day needs. Each Buddy committed to a year's service to clients. Besides emotional support, the Buddies connected clients with social service agencies and offered help with shopping, dog walking, and apartment cleaning. GMHC found mental health experts to conduct therapy sessions for gay couples in which only one partner was infected. Lawyers offered free advice on making wills. The GMHC also became a fixture in New York's fund-raising calendar. Its 1985 art auction at Sotheby's was the first AIDS-related charity event to raise more than $1 million.

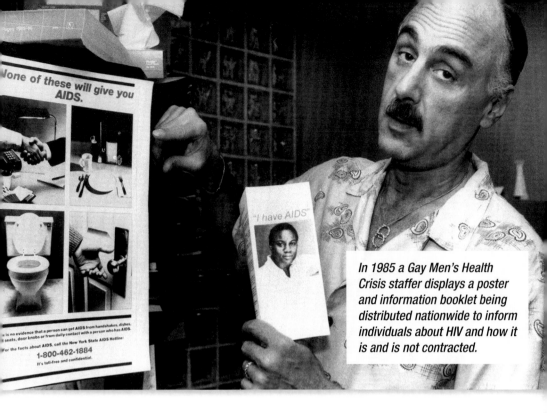

None of these will give you AIDS.

There is no evidence that a person can get AIDS from handshakes, dishes, toilet seats, door knobs or from daily contact with a person who has AIDS.

For the facts about AIDS, call the New York State AIDS Hotline:

1-800-462-1884

It's toll-free and confidential.

"I have AIDS"

In 1985 a Gay Men's Health Crisis staffer displays a poster and information booklet being distributed nationwide to inform individuals about HIV and how it is and is not contracted.

Advocating for Safe Sex

The GMHC led the way in calling for safe sex. During the 1980s public references to condoms and how to use them were still rare. Yet Kramer and other leaders of the GMHC knew that using condoms was crucial to limiting the spread of AIDS and saving lives. In widely distributed pamphlets, the GMHC not only urged condom usage but also recommended a serious discussion about using them before engaging in a sexual encounter. The 1983 pamphlet *How to Have Sex in an Epidemic* includes this advice:

> Safe sex does not require that you know your partner well, but it usually requires that you both agree before you have sex what you will and will not do. . . . If a potential partner becomes defensive or critical of your health concerns, it's probably because he feels you are implying that he might give you a disease. Since this is exactly what you are implying, be polite and move on. Find a partner who will be reassured by your concerns—not put off by them.[15]

This approach to negotiating safe sex procedures has influenced today's concerns about affirmative consent and safe sex. The GMHC pamphlets also addressed the hot-button topic of anonymous sex in public places like gay bathhouses, bookstores, and private clubs. The charge that reckless promiscuity among gay men was fueling the AIDS crisis was difficult to dismiss. Spokespersons in the gay community insisted that the issue mainly served as a smoke screen for fear and discrimination. Nonetheless, public health officials began to act. On October 10, 1984, the city of San Francisco filed a lawsuit against bathhouse operators, citing their businesses as a public nuisance. Owners were ordered to employ monitors to prevent unsafe sex on the premises, as well as remove most doors and barriers to private booths, rooms, or cubicles. Rather than relinquish privacy protections, all the bathhouses in San Francisco closed.

Gay activists denounced the lawsuit as discriminatory. They suggested it would be better if bathhouses remained open and were employed as sources of information about safe sex procedures. But a newspaper poll found that 79 percent of San Franciscans disagreed. Even sympathetic Democrats like then-mayor of San Francisco Dianne Feinstein supported the closings to save lives. Nationally, some pundits began to worry that the virus would break out into the general population. At the end of 1984, as total AIDS deaths reached 3,665 in the United States, political tensions about the disease threatened to boil over.

A Death Changes the Narrative

Activists directed their frustrations about AIDS to the federal government. President Ronald Reagan, a California conservative, had not publicly referred to the disease since he had taken office in 1980. Asked about the growing AIDS epidemic in which one out of three people infected were dying, Reagan's press secretary, Larry Speakes, pretended not to know what AIDS was. Gay protesters angrily demanded to know why the government was doing nothing to find a cure. In a March 1983 essay, Kramer had pointed out that the government spent $10 million to investigate seven deaths from cyanide-laced Tylenol, yet not one dollar had been dedicated to AIDS research. As Kramer declared, "If this article doesn't rouse you to anger, fury, rage, and action, gay men have no future on this planet."[16]

To most Americans at the time, HIV/AIDS was a disease that affected only marginalized groups in the shadows. On July 25, 1985, however, a startling disclosure began to change that narrative. Publicists revealed that actor Rock Hudson had contracted AIDS. Hudson, known for his many romantic movie and television

The Ryan White Case

The deaths of celebrities like Rock Hudson, rock singer Freddie Mercury, and dancer Rudolf Nureyev helped change public perceptions about AIDS. But others with the disease often met with fear and discrimination. Ryan White was thirteen years old when he was diagnosed with HIV in December 1984. The teen from Kokomo, Indiana, was one of the first children and first hemophiliacs to contract HIV. He got the virus from a blood transfusion during treatment for hemophilia. Once his condition became public, White faced opposition from parents and other students when he tried to return to school. Some assumed that he was gay and called his infection a punishment from God. "I was labeled a troublemaker, my mom an unfit mother, and I was not welcome anywhere," said White. "Because of the lack of education on AIDS, discrimination, fear, panic, and lies surrounded me."

Ryan and his mother's battle to get him back into school made national headlines. Eventually, the family moved to Cicero, Indiana, where sympathetic students had taken time to educate fellow students, parents, and neighbors about HIV/AIDS. White was able to live the normal life of a teenager. He died of AIDS-related pneumonia on April 8, 1990.

Quoted in Liz Meszaros, "On This Day in Medical History: Ryan White Succumbs to AIDS-Related Pneumonia," MDLinx, April 4, 2018. www.mdlinx.com.

roles, had been regarded as a heterosexual role model. By the time he died, on October 2, 1985, *People* magazine and other sources had thoroughly detailed his secret gay life.

In mourning his old Hollywood friend, Reagan acknowledged the scourge of AIDS for the first time. The death from AIDS of such a popular celebrity caused many to change their views of the disease's victims. In addition, Hudson was revealed to be a strong supporter of research into HIV/AIDS. His coming out as gay and subsequent death brought new attention to fund-raising drives. As *People* reported in December 1985, "Since Hudson made his announcement, more than $1.8 million in private contributions (more than double the amount collected in 1984) has been raised to support AIDS research and to care for AIDS victims (5,523 reported in 1985 alone). A few days after Hudson died, Congress set aside $221 million to develop a cure for AIDS."[17]

Fighting for Rights and a Cure

Despite some progress, widespread paranoia about AIDS persisted in the United States. In June 1986 the US Department of Justice ruled that businesses could fire workers with AIDS merely on the grounds that their presence might cause emotional distress in other employees. Conservative columnist William F. Buckley proposed that gay men with HIV should be tattooed on the buttocks to warn away possible sex partners. Eccentric California multimillionaire Lyndon LaRouche formed a group called PANIC whose goal was to set up quarantine camps for people with AIDS. A petition drive for the group gathered more than seven hundred thousand signatures. At the same time, brutal beatings of gay men were reported in San Francisco and other cities.

In response to the alarmist climate in the United States, certain gay activists decided to organize. Led by the fiery Kramer—who had been fired from the GMHC for his radicalism—these people fought against antigay bigotry and demanded research on a cure for AIDS. Unlike other organizations, however, this new group would unleash edgy and outrageous protests designed to gain maximum attention whatever the cost. A male nurse at one of the early meetings came up with the name: AIDS Coalition to Unleash Power, or ACT UP. Members wore T-shirts emblazoned with a pink triangle and the motto Silence = Death. The desperate need for effective AIDS treatment drove the group's frenetic activity. As David France, a historian of the AIDS activist movement, declares, "It's also hard to remember that on the night ACT UP was founded, in 1987—six years into the epidemic and 15,000 American deaths later—there was still not a single pill on

Angry about the federal government's response to the AIDS crisis, members of ACT UP protest in front of the FDA offices in 1988. Protests by this group were aimed at gaining maximum attention.

the market to prescribe. It sure seemed likely that every gay man would perish without a tear from the rest of the world."[18] Over the next decade, ACT UP would expand to include ten thousand members in nineteen countries.

The group's assaults on proper society outraged many while inspiring others. Hundreds of ACT UP members gathered in city streets to stage so-called die-ins. Lying on the pavement and refusing to budge, they would halt traffic until the police arrived. Chanting slogans and carrying signs, they held demonstrations on Wall Street and managed to shut down Grand Central Terminal. Small bands burst into health care offices and sprayed fake blood on the office computers. They descended on pharmaceutical company cocktail parties in swanky hotel ballrooms, chanting and overturning tables. Their most notorious gambit was to disrupt services at New York City's St. Patrick's Cathedral in protest of Cardinal O'Connor's opposition to condom use.

"On the night ACT UP was founded, in 1987—six years into the epidemic and 15,000 American deaths later—there was still not a single pill on the market to prescribe [for AIDS treatment]."[18]

—David France, a historian of the AIDS activist movement

The First Effective Treatments

ACT UP members also armed themselves with facts and statistics to bolster their demands. They would barge into federal offices, like the National Institutes of Health, ready with genuine proposals about boosting AIDS research. One of their main goals was to speed up the procedure for testing promising new drug treatments. "What made this work was not just the anger," says France. "But the anger coupled with the intelligence. What they were able to revolutionize was really the very way that [anti-AIDS] drugs are identified and tested."[19]

Whether or not due to ACT UP tactics, the concentrated efforts of AIDS researchers began to bear fruit. In March 1987 the US Food and Drug Administration (FDA) gave approval for azidothymidine (AZT), the first antiretroviral drug, for treatment of HIV. A decade later, in September 1997, the FDA approved Combivir, a treatment that was effective and easy to use. With Combivir, a combination of two antiretroviral drugs, HIV-positive people could control their disease by taking a single tablet every day.

As HIV/AIDS infections spread, gay activists took to the streets to fight bigotry and demand private and governmental action on finding a cure. Activists also organized groups like the GMHC to support AIDS sufferers with accurate information and better standards of care. Their efforts became a model for political action that is still influential today.

CHAPTER THREE

The AIDS Crisis in Africa

In 1987 two doctors in the African nation of Uganda set out to investigate an epidemic in the rural district of Rakai, located in the southwest. They had received reports of a particularly severe outbreak of what the locals called "slim disease." The baffling illness, which had been circulating in the country for at least five years, caused high fever and diarrhea. Its victims, both women and men, would shed pounds at an alarming rate, leaving them rail-thin and very weak. The sight of such skeletal people in a country that values heft and curves was unnerving. Many victims also developed infections like Kaposi's sarcoma. Contracting slim disease tended to be a death sentence, with most patients dying in a matter of weeks or months. Among rural Ugandans, rumors spread that witchcraft was the cause. But the true culprit proved to be the AIDS virus.

Linked to HIV

The two doctors, David Serwadda and Nelson Sewankambo, studied the people and daily life of Rakai in detail. They finally identified slim disease as a form of HIV, the first known cases in the country. It resembled the wasting syndrome reported in AIDS patients in the West. Their discovery perplexed Serwadda. As he recalled, "We just could not connect a disease in white, homosexual males in San Francisco to the thing that we were staring at."[20]

To further their research, they set up a tiny clinic in a rented hotel room in the town of Kyotera. The makeshift facility depended on a 40-watt bulb for light—when electricity was available—and a hand centrifuge for spinning blood samples. Yet Serwadda and Sewankambo performed world-class research at the site, eventually partnering with both the National Institutes of Health and the CDC in the United States. They also treated patients with HIV and advised people on prevention methods. According to Nuala McGovern, a New York radio producer who traveled to Rakai, "The area became the epicenter of HIV and AIDS in Uganda, both in cases and research, and even slipped [into] Ugandan vernacular. If you wanted to insult someone, calling them 'Rakai' or 'Slim' was an effective way."[21] McGovern noted that locally elected health officials would travel to Rakai to get the latest facts on HIV/AIDS prevention. Then they would carry the information back to their village councils.

> "We just could not connect a disease in white, homosexual males in San Francisco to the thing that we were staring at."[20]
>
> —David Serwadda, a Ugandan doctor

An Explosion of AIDS Cases

The AIDS crisis in Africa dwarfs the numbers in the rest of the world. With about 15 percent of the world's population, today the continent holds more than two-thirds of those with HIV/AIDS infections. The rate of infection in some southern African nations—such as Botswana, Namibia, South Africa, and Zambia—can be one hundred times higher than in the United States. Unlike the United States, where AIDS has remained chiefly a disease of gay men and IV drug users, African nations face an AIDS pandemic that mostly affects the heterosexual population.

Why AIDS cases have exploded in Africa—and especially in the sub-Saharan region—has sparked much debate among researchers. No single cause seems to explain the extent of the crisis.

Researchers have suggested that everything from cultural differences to sexual habits to genetic variations are responsible. One theory holds that migrant laborers, with their perpetual movement, use of prostitutes, and multiple sex partners, have played a key role in spreading the virus. Studies have pointed to high rates of polygamy, or multiple spouses, as a cause. Some scientists believe that the African continent is host to especially virulent strains of HIV, making infections more frequent and more deadly. Others theorize that Africans have a gene, developed to resist malaria, that makes them more vulnerable to HIV and slow to display its symptoms. This combination could lead infected persons to spread the virus unwittingly.

The failure to find one overall root cause has frustrated researchers in Africa. But that failure might have a silver lining. "One of the big breakthroughs that has so advanced the fight against AIDS in Africa was when everyone seemed to realize that perhaps the best approach, even if it's frustrating and complicated and difficult, is piecemeal," says Max Fisher, who writes on geopolitics for the

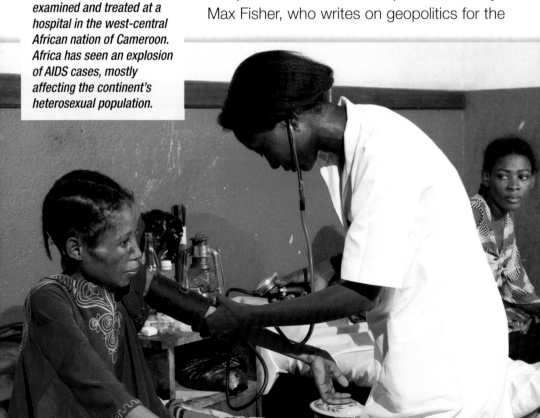

An HIV/AIDS patient is examined and treated at a hospital in the west-central African nation of Cameroon. Africa has seen an explosion of AIDS cases, mostly affecting the continent's heterosexual population.

Atlantic. "It might not be very satisfying or exciting to launch a thousand tiny programs, but it's what's worked."[22]

Death of a President's Son

Before programs could be launched, however, leaders had to acknowledge that the problem existed. In the mid-1980s many African leaders—especially those in sub-Saharan Africa, where the spread was greatest—denied that HIV was infecting growing numbers of their people. They feared that the stigma attached to the disease would discourage commerce and hurt their countries' economies. Health experts believe that this delay in acknowledging the epidemic led to higher infection rates and more deaths.

In October 1987 a startling admission by an African leader began to change attitudes about HIV/AIDS. Kenneth D. Kaunda, president of Zambia, announced that his son's death the previous year had been related to AIDS. Thirty-year-old Masuzgo Gwebe Kaunda had died of liver and kidney failure following a long illness. The president's statement brought into the open a disease often spoken about in nervous whispers. Researchers at the time estimated that 20 percent of Zambia's population was infected with HIV. Kaunda also declared AIDS to be a global threat. "It does not need my son's death to appeal to the international community to treat the question of AIDS as a world problem," Kaunda said at a news conference. "It is something that is so serious, that once again I plead with the World Health Organization and those in a position to help fund the campaign against AIDS. We want to fight this together, regardless of who dies from it."[23]

Shining a spotlight on the AIDS crisis in Africa may have been Kaunda's greatest hour. In 1991, after ruling Zambia for twenty-seven years as a dictator, he lost in a free election by

> "One of the big breakthroughs that has so advanced the fight against AIDS in Africa was when everyone seemed to realize that perhaps the best approach, even if it's frustrating and complicated and difficult, is piecemeal."[22]
>
> —Max Fisher, a reporter on geopolitics for the *Atlantic*

a landslide. Kaunda went on to found the South Africa–based Children of Africa Foundation, which promoted education for orphans of AIDS victims and raised funds for AIDS medications across the continent. Kaunda lost another son to AIDS-related illness in 2005.

That same year, former South African president Nelson Mandela offered another boost to AIDS awareness in Africa. In January he broke one of his country's taboos about AIDS by openly admitting that his own son, Makgatho, had died of the disease in a Johannesburg clinic. Mandela, hugely respected worldwide, hoped to bring Africa's AIDS crisis out of the shadows. "Let us give publicity to HIV/AIDS and not hide it," he said, "because the only way of making it appear to be a normal illness just like TB, like cancer, is always to come out and say somebody has died because of HIV."[24]

> "Let us give publicity to HIV/AIDS and not hide it."[24]
>
> —Nelson Mandela, an apartheid opponent and former president of South Africa

Denial and Policy Failures in South Africa

South Africa had become one of the worst hot spots for HIV/AIDS since the disease had emerged there in 1982. During the 1980s the nation was focused on the struggle to dismantle apartheid, the White government's system of racial discrimination and separation. With political battles raging, less notice was given to HIV, which broke out among the Black townships and the gay community. In 1990, as Black South Africans celebrated Mandela's release after twenty-seven years in prison, the nation's infection rate for HIV was still less than 1 percent.

During the 1990s, however, HIV/AIDS infections began to skyrocket in South Africa. During Mandela's five-year presidency from 1994 to 1999, government officials repeatedly denied the seriousness of the problem. Mandela would later admit that his failure to confront the epidemic was a major mistake. At century's end, South Africa had the world's largest number of HIV infections, with 22.4 percent of the population living with the virus.

Under Mandela's successor, Thabo Mbeki, the crisis only got worse. Mbeki ignored officials of his Department of Health when they submitted a rigorous five-year plan to fight the disease. He repeatedly rejected donations of AIDS drugs from Western nations. Instead of effective drugs, Mbeki's health minister recommended beetroot, garlic, and African potatoes as treatment. While hosting the International AIDS Conference in Durban, Mbeki announced he was skeptical that HIV causes AIDS. Instead, he blamed the outbreak on poverty and poor nourishment. By 2005 more than nine hundred South Africans were dying each day of AIDS-related illness. In 2008 researchers at Harvard University concluded that Mbeki's misguided policies had directly caused more than 330,000 unnecessary AIDS deaths in South Africa.

"Access to appropriate public health practice is often determined by a small number of political leaders," declared Harvard scientist Pride Chigwedere. "In the case of

Surrounded by family, Nelson Mandela talks to the media in 2005 about the death of his son from AIDS. By speaking publicly, Mandela hoped to bring Africa's AIDS crisis out of the shadows.

South Africa, many lives were lost because of a failure to accept the use of available ARVs [antiretroviral drugs] to prevent and treat HIV/AIDS in a timely manner."[25]

The Treatment Action Campaign

It took the combined efforts of activists in South Africa to turn the tide on AIDS treatment. On December 10, 1998, a diverse group of fifteen people gathered on the steps of St. George's Cathedral in Cape Town. They demanded government action to provide medical treatment for AIDS victims. Among the group were activists, people with HIV, a former human rights official, a medical student, and a sympathetic grandmother. They expressed outrage that South Africans continued to die unnecessarily from AIDS, when other countries were treating the disease with great success. Passersby were surprised to learn that effective drugs for AIDS even existed, let alone that they were widely available in Europe and the United States. That day, the group on the cathedral steps managed to collect more than one thousand signatures on a bold petition. It called for the government to set up a treatment program for people with HIV.

The group used its petition to create the Treatment Action Campaign (TAC). TAC brought a new energy to AIDS politics across South Africa. People had been demoralized by gloomy forecasts: that millions would die from AIDS, the health care system would collapse, and the economy would falter. Even health workers and AIDS activists had assumed that developing countries like South Africa could not afford the latest treatments. TAC rejected these claims and offered hope that the disease could be stopped in its tracks.

One of TAC's organizers was Zackie Achmat, a former activist against apartheid. "I had been thinking about treatment for a while and asking how we

> "I had been thinking about [AIDS] treatment for a while and asking how we could stand by and do nothing while people kept dying."[26]
>
> —Zackie Achmat, an activist who helped start the Treatment Action Campaign in South Africa

40

Safer Sex with Circumcision

Promoting safe sex and fewer extramarital relationships has been effective in reducing the spread of HIV in Uganda. A less obvious proposal has also achieved success: male circumcision, or removing the foreskin. "It's probably the oldest and most common form of surgery," says radio producer Nuala McGovern. "Scientists suggest it's effective because cells inside the foreskin are an ideal breeding ground for the virus and allow it [to] be passed on during sexual intercourse. Cut them out, and the breeding ground is gone." During intercourse, the foreskin is also prone to small scratches and tears that can lead to transmission by blood. Researchers say the risk of HIV infection is two to eight times higher for uncircumcised men.

In the Ugandan district of Rakai, the surgery room where circumcisions are performed usually has a steady line of waiting patients. Males from infants to older adults are candidates for the procedure. Across Uganda the ratio of doctors to patients is roughly one to eighteen thousand. As a result, health officials have considered enlisting non-surgeons to perform the fairly simple procedure. They intend to continue the program since trials at the Rakai clinic suggest it decreases HIV by 51 percent.

Nuala McGovern, "Outposts: Men, Cross Your Legs," WNYC, May 8, 2008. www.wnyc.org.

could stand by and do nothing while people kept dying," says Achmat. "But whoever I spoke to said it was impossible; the drugs were way out of our reach."[26] When Achmat himself developed severe illness from AIDS, his life was saved only because his friends helped him pay for an expensive drug. Even so, he nearly was bankrupted. He realized that thousands like him were dying needlessly every day. His impassioned speech at a friend's funeral led to the gathering at the Cape Town cathedral in 1998.

Mbeki posed the main obstacle to TAC's rallying cry for AIDS treatment. In 2002 the group won a landmark court case forcing the government to make antiretroviral drugs available to pregnant women with HIV. In February 2003 TAC staged a huge march outside the parliament building where Mbeki was making his state of the nation speech. Several of Mbeki's political opponents wore TAC's HIV Positive T-shirts to the president's speech. When Mbeki was forced from office in 2008, TAC expanded its influence in

South Africa and across the sub-Saharan region. Till then, most surrounding nations had also failed to slow the outbreak. In Botswana one-third of all sexually active adults had HIV. HIV/AIDS had become the number one killer in southern Africa. Yet TAC's tireless work to obtain practical AIDS treatment gave HIV/AIDS victims new hope in their struggle with the disease. According to South Africa's Medical Research Council, life expectancy in South Africa jumped from fifty-three years in 2005 to sixty-two years in 2015.

Uganda's "Love Carefully" Campaign

Meanwhile, the site of David Serwadda and Nelson Sewankambo's early research had developed into a surprising AIDS success story. Beginning in the late 1980s, Uganda promoted a widespread campaign for safe sex. The slogans Love Carefully and Zero Grazing were posted on billboards and buildings around the country.

The slogans meant "use condoms" and "do not have sexual partners outside your marriage." (*Grazing* is Ugandan slang for "extramarital sex.") The campaign also urged abstinence for young people, especially teenage girls, and provided information about how the disease was transmitted. Researchers found that rates of casual sex dropped by 60 percent from 1989 to 1995, leading to sharp declines in rates of HIV infection. Health experts disagree

Posters like this one in Uganda are part of an HIV/AIDS prevention campaign urging young men to practice safe sex.

on the true reasons for such declines. Some believe the key was getting the problem discussed in the open. Ugandan males, who often carried on two or three concurrent sexual relationships on their travels, may have been influenced to get tested more often for HIV and to take other precautions. And the struggle is ongoing, since HIV/AIDS remains a serious health crisis in Uganda.

The AIDS crisis in Africa began with observation of people wasting away with the slim disease in Uganda and other countries. Research showed that HIV had already taken hold in many regions of the continent. Reluctance to speak about the disease or confront it with government action helped HIV/AIDS tighten its grip on African nations, particularly in the sub-Saharan area. Only when national leaders like Zambia's Kenneth D. Kaunda acknowledged the problem did attitudes begin to change. Activists in South Africa started TAC to obtain the latest drug treatments for AIDS victims. Uganda and other African nations found success with initiatives for testing, safe sex, and abstinence. As Nkululeko Nxesi, former head of a South African AIDS care organization, says, "Down the line, we will realize that development is not only about how good your infrastructure is, but it's also about the heart."[27]

CHAPTER FOUR

Living with H1V/A1DS Today

The first treatment for AIDS to meet with even partial success was based on a failure. The drug AZT had first been developed in the 1960s as a cancer-targeting treatment for chemotherapy patients. But in the 1980s, with scientists making a desperate search through abandoned drugs for something to combat AIDS, AZT got a second look. At the time, new cases of HIV/AIDS and deaths from the virus were doubling about every year. Patients, most in the prime of their lives, were willing to try anything. AZT was an antiretroviral drug that seemed to prevent HIV from copying itself and multiplying. Rushed into controlled trials, it showed some ability to increase CD4 white blood cell counts, strengthening the user's immune system. Robert Yarchoan, one of AZT's developers for AIDS treatment at the drug firm Burroughs Wellcome, remembers his team's breakthrough. "I think we doubled the dose," he recalls. "And six out of six patients at that dose had an increase in their CD4 cells. . . . We were, at that point, very, very excited that we really had something."[28]

Experts hailed the drug's discovery as a major breakthrough in treating AIDS. On March 19, 1987, the FDA gave AZT a fast-track approval. The whole process, which usually took an average of eight to ten years, had been completed in twenty months.

No Magic Bullet

AZT was far from the so-called magic bullet to cure AIDS, as patients had hoped. Despite the hype, doctors never said it was a cure. At most, they referred to it as a light at the end of the tunnel. It seemed to prolong life by about one year—a great boon for those facing AIDS as a death sentence. But its drawbacks began to multiply. To begin with, AZT had a large price tag: about $8,000 a year (more than $18,000 in today's money). The boost it offered to the immune system was slight, and after only eight weeks patients began to develop resistance. Moreover, the drug's side effects were devastating. Patients suffered severe headaches, nausea, and muscle fatigue. Tests done by medical researchers in Great Britain and France found that HIV-positive patients received no benefits from taking AZT before the onset of full-blown AIDS. Death rates were higher for the test group that took the drug than for the control group that only took a placebo, or fake pill. John Lauritzen, a writer for a gay newspaper in New York, discovered that the American trials for the drug had been filled with errors and confusion. Discerning the genuine pills by taste, test subjects had shared their doses of the drug with the placebo group, making the test results meaningless.

> "I think we doubled the dose. And six out of six patients at that dose had an increase in their CD4 cells. . . . We were, at that point, very, very excited that we really had something."[28]
>
> —Robert Yarchoan, one of the developers of AZT as an AIDS treatment

Some patients felt betrayed by all the false claims for AZT. Michael Cottrell, an Englishman who tested positive for HIV in the mid-1980s, took the drug because at the time there was no alternative. He soon learned that many problems with AZT were due to prescriptions that overdid the dosage. "Intuitively, I didn't think it was doing me any good," he says. "I was prescribed it three times over a period of three years, and I took it out of fear. I was first prescribed 1,200 mg a day, and then 500 mg, but I still felt bad, even on the lower dose. I had nausea and headaches and

46

muscle fatigue."[29] Cottrell got used to carrying around a large bag filled with pill containers. Fortunately, for those like Cottrell whose infection had yet to develop into full-blown AIDS, more effective drugs were on the way.

An Effective Combination of Drugs

The next important breakthrough in AIDS research was a class of drugs called protease inhibitors. They block the activity of protease enzymes, which enable HIV to multiply. In other words, they interrupt the life cycle of HIV. Like AZT, they stop the virus from copying itself. The first protease inhibitor drug, called saquinavir, won FDA approval in December 1995. Upon its release, life expectancy for AIDS patients rose immediately. Research scientists began to suggest that protease inhibitors might be a revolutionary treatment. They were the result of what is called rational drug design, using knowledge of molecules to find medications that react with biological targets in desired ways. As Roy Gulick, a doctor who ran clinical trials for the drugs at New York's Cornell

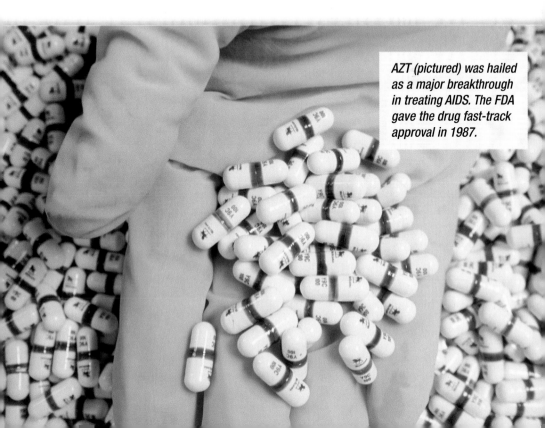

AZT (pictured) was hailed as a major breakthrough in treating AIDS. The FDA gave the drug fast-track approval in 1987.

University, noted at the time, "We may finally have the tools to turn HIV infection into a long-term, manageable and treatable disease, much like hypertension and diabetes."[30]

Even better news for AIDS victims soon arrived. Researchers discovered that combination therapies far outperformed any single drug for controlling HIV. For example, AZT proved to be more effective when used along with a protease inhibitor like saquinavir. Studies began to affirm the insight of David Barry, Burroughs Wellcome's leading virology expert. "You're going to have four or five drugs for the OIs [opportunistic infections] and two, three and maybe four drugs for antivirals,"[31] said Barry.

The new treatment regimen, introduced in 1996, was called highly active antiretroviral therapy (HAART). This was not a stop-gap measure like AZT had been. HAART offered hope that the lives of people with HIV/AIDS could be extended indefinitely—that a person could live a relatively normal life with HIV. At first, HAART

Enlisting More Women for AIDS Research

More than half of the world's 35 million people living with HIV are women. Yet clinical trials of AIDS treatments and possible vaccines tend to include few females. A 2016 study found that only 11 percent of subjects in cure trials were women. And females made up less than 20 percent of participants in trials of antiretroviral drugs. This is a key shortcoming, since women are known to react to HIV infection much differently than men.

For example, when first diagnosed, women tend to have lower viral loads, or amount of HIV in the blood, than men at the same stage. Females with HIV are much less likely to develop severe infections like Kaposi's sarcoma. A woman's immune system tends to control the virus for five to seven years. But afterward, women progress to full-blown AIDS more rapidly than HIV-positive men and are more likely to suffer strokes and heart attacks. These differences are crucial to research on cures for AIDS. "If we're going to find a cure," says Rowena Johnston, director of research for the charity amfAR, "it's important that we find a cure that actually works for everybody."

Quoted in Apoorva Mandavilli, "Half of H.I.V. Patients Are Women. Most Research Subjects Are Men," *New York Times*, May 28, 2019. www.nytimes.com.

Although there is still no cure for AIDS, people like former basketball star Magic Johnson have been able to live full lives for decades despite being HIV-positive.

treatment required patients to take a bewildering assortment of pills every day. Confusion over doses and troublesome side effects caused many early HAART patients to abandon the therapy. But in 1997 the FDA approved the medication Combivir, which combined AZT with saquinavir in a single pill and was much easier to take. HAART drugs became known as a cocktail of AIDS treatments carefully designed to keep the virus at bay. By reducing the viral load of HIV while raising the CD4 white blood cell count, these drugs keep pushing the threat of full-blown AIDS further into the distance. There is still no cure for the disease. Nonetheless, people like former basketball star Magic Johnson have been able to live full lives for decades despite being HIV positive.

The patent for AZT expired in 2005. Since then, several generic forms of the drug have appeared, which is rare for HIV treatments.

A constant influx of new AIDS drugs with patents keeps costs high (not to mention pharmaceutical company profits). Studies show that the lifetime cost of treating an HIV infection is about $380,000. For people with lower CD4 counts—that is, weaker immune systems—the cost can be much higher.

Living with HIV

Due to treatment advances like HAART, people with HIV today can expect to live nearly as long as the average person. Much depends on the patient's CD4 numbers and viral load. The US Department of Health and Human Services (HHS) recommends that an HIV-positive person get tested for CD4 counts every twelve months. CD4 testing is optional if the person's count is above five hundred cells per milliliter. The HHS recommends testing for viral load every three to four months for patients with stable immune systems. Viral load is the key barometer for the success of antiretroviral treatment

A Pill to Prevent HIV Infections

People who consider themselves at risk for getting HIV can now take a pill to prevent infection. Truvada, which was first approved by the FDA in 2012, provides pre-exposure prophylaxis, or PrEP for short. It not only controls HIV in people who are already infected but also is up to 99 percent effective in preventing a user from getting HIV. The drug is used mostly by gay or bisexual men who have had sex without a condom in the past six months.

For all its potential, Truvada has yet to be as widely adopted as originally hoped. The drug is expensive and must be taken daily for maximum protection. Critics also fear that Truvada provides high-risk users with a false sense of security. They warn that the drug could lead to less use of condoms and an increase in spread of other sexually transmitted diseases. Nonetheless, the PrEP approach has nearly wiped out HIV infections in Australia and reduced infections in New York to historic lows. According to John Brooks, senior medical adviser at the CDC, "There's a lot of interest in what we can do with PrEP to meet consumers where they are, find the right formulation for each type of consumer."

Quoted in Sara Harrison, "PrEP Made HIV Prevention Easier—and It's Getting Simpler," *Wired,* July 30, 2019. www.wired.com.

(ART). Those living with the virus face increasing risks from other ailments as well. As HIV-positive people age, they are at greater risk of developing cardiovascular disease, lung disease, cancer, liver disease (including hepatitis B and C), and other infections.

Being HIV positive does not prevent a person from living a normal life. Medically, an infected person must take one pill a day for ART and make frequent doctor visits. The doctor must be informed about any unusual symptoms. Vaccinations can also help prevent other infections. If a person with HIV suspects an infection or develops a fever, treatment should be sought immediately, including antibiotics or antifungal drugs. Food poisoning can be more serious for HIV-positive individuals, even life threatening in some cases, so extra care should be taken with handling and preparing food. Use of tobacco, alcohol, or narcotics is best avoided. Otherwise, these persons can do almost anything uninfected people can. Living with someone who is HIV positive need not be especially dangerous either. Experts say a spouse or partner should get regular tests and the couple should practice safe sex techniques.

> "I'm the face of HIV. . . . You probably know someone who is HIV positive, you just don't know that they're HIV positive."[32]
>
> —Richard Cordova, an HIV-positive spin instructor

In 2011, ABC News reported on Richard Cordova, then age thirty-three, for a project called A Day with HIV in America. Cordova's weekly routine revealed that being HIV positive does not require a person to be a shut-in. Two days a week, Cordova rose early to teach a 6:00 a.m. spin class. He had completed seven marathons, three bike tours of more than 200 miles (322 km), and a triathlon. Cordova insisted his strenuous lifestyle was nothing extraordinary. "I'm the face of HIV," Cordova said. "It could be the person serving you your coffee, the child at school that sits next to your child, the person who's cutting your hair, your co-worker. You probably know someone who is HIV positive, you just don't know that they're HIV positive."[32] Today more than 2 million Americans are living with HIV, with 40,000 more infections occurring each year. Health officials estimate that 14 percent of HIV-positive individuals are unaware of their condition. All told, nearly 700,000 Americans have died of AIDS and AIDS-related illness.

Safe Sex and Screening

Aside from antiretroviral drug treatments, the main approach to managing AIDS has been the campaign for safe sex. This includes having protected sex during every sexual encounter. The CDC recommends using a male or female condom during vaginal or anal sex. It also urges use of a condom or dental dam for oral sex. A male condom is a latex sheath that fits over the penis. A female condom is a loose-fitting latex pouch that is inserted into the vagina. Both are used to prevent the exchange of bodily fluids during intercourse, which can result in HIV infection. In the late 1980s, groups like the GMHC and ACT UP began distributing condoms at public events and encouraging education about safe sex in schools and recreation centers. Despite opposition from religious leaders and social conservatives, campaigns for safe sex steadily gained public acceptance. Supplying condoms, both male and female versions, and educating young people about safe sex procedures has helped nations around the world address the raging AIDS pandemic. However, health officials stress that condom usage is not foolproof for preventing HIV transmission. Condoms can tear or leak and often are not used correctly. The only certain way to avoid HIV/AIDS is abstinence, or not having sex.

Another method for preventing the spread of HIV has proved even more controversial, at least in Western countries. Screening people at risk for AIDS with antibody tests—which became available as far back as 1985—was intended to keep HIV-positive people from putting others in danger during sexual encounters. Yet many refused to be tested, fearing the stigma attached to having HIV or even being screened for the virus. There was no effective treatment for the disease, so to many at risk, testing seemed hopeless. "The only thing that could happen would be

Aside from drug treatments, the main approach to managing AIDS has been the campaign for safe sex. Public health officials urge people to use condoms as the primary means of practicing safe sex.

getting fired from your job or kicked out by your roommate or disowned by your family," says Mark S. King, who received a positive test for HIV in 1985. "None of the outcomes were good."[33]

The CDC recommends that all people ages thirteen to sixty-four get tested for HIV at least once. Those who have unprotected sex or inject drugs should get regular tests. People can go to a doctor's office or clinic to get reliable tests. After years of delays, the FDA finally approved the first in-home HIV test, called OraQuick, in 2012. The OraQuick test uses oral fluids to test for HIV antibodies.

> "The only thing that could happen would be getting fired from your job or kicked out by your roommate or disowned by your family. None of the outcomes were good."[33]
>
> —Mark S. King, a man who tested positive for HIV in 1985

PEPFAR and Beyond

A notable success in the global battle against HIV/AIDS is the President's Emergency Plan for AIDS Relief, or PEPFAR. This anti-HIV foreign aid program was started by the George W. Bush administration in 2003 and has been renewed several times since. As the largest global health initiative targeting a single disease in history, PEPFAR has saved more than 18 million lives and prevented millions of infections worldwide. Over its history, the program has spent more than $80 billion on treating, preventing, and researching HIV/AIDS. As of 2020, PEPFAR had provided antiretroviral therapy to 16.5 million women, men, and children and sponsored 24.5 million medical male circumcisions. Recently, PEPFAR partnered with districts in Zimbabwe, Malawi, and Lesotho to reduce new HIV cases in adolescent girls and young women by 25 percent.

Despite PEPFAR's accomplishments, much more needs to be done. Young people need to be educated about the dangers of unprotected sex and other risky behaviors. Still, as noted by Deborah L. Birx, coordinator of US government activities to combat HIV/AIDS, PEPFAR continues to play a crucial role in responding to infectious disease, including COVID-19. "It's the platforms that we've built together," says Birx, "and the [community] relationships that are going to be our solutions not only for HIV, but our response to COVID-19 around the world."[34]

Breakthroughs in treating AIDS have enabled HIV-positive individuals to live nearly normal lives. From the approval of the first antiretroviral drug, AZT, in 1987 to the discovery of protease inhibitor drugs and combination therapies, AIDS treatment has continued to advance. While HIV/AIDS is no longer the death sentence it once was, researchers still hope to find a cure for this physically and socially damaging disease.

SOURCE NOTES

Introduction: An Ongoing Battle Against HIV

1. Quoted in World Health Organization, "The Cost of Inaction: COVID-19-Related Service Disruptions Could Cause Hundreds of Thousands of Extra Deaths from HIV," May 11, 2020. www.who.int.
2. Quoted in Jen Christensen, "AIDS in the '80s: The Rise of a New Civil Rights Movement," CNN, June 1, 2016. www.cnn.com.
3. Deborah L. Birx and Brett P. Giroir, "ICYMI—Ending the HIV/AIDS Epidemic: Community by Community," HIV .gov, November 27, 2019. www.hiv.gov.

Chapter One: The Origins of HIV

4. Quoted in Nelson Vergel, "There When AIDS Began: An Interview with Michael Gottlieb, M.D.," TheBodyPro, June 2, 2011. www.thebodypro.com.
5. Lawrence K. Altman, "Rare Cancer Seen in 41 Homosexuals," *New York Times*, July 3, 1981. www.nytimes.com.
6. Robert Bazell, "Dispute Behind Nobel Prize for HIV Research," NBC News, October 6, 2008. www.nbcnews .com.
7. Quoted in Merrill Fabry, "This Is How the HIV Test Was Invented," *Time*, June 27, 2016. www.time.com.
8. Quoted in Devin Dwyer, "U.S. Ban on HIV-Positive Visitors, Immigrants Expires," ABC News, January 5, 2010. www.abcnews.com.
9. Quoted in Simon Garfield, "Jonathan Grimshaw: 'I Tested HIV Positive in 1984'," *The Guardian* (Manchester, UK), February 5, 2011. www.theguardian.com.
10. Claudia Wallis, "AIDS: A Growing Threat," *Time*, August 12, 1985. http://content.time.com.

Chapter Two: Solidarity and Stigma

11. Quoted in Nurith Aizenman, "How to Demand a Medical Breakthrough: Lessons from the AIDS Fight," NPR, February 9, 2019. www.npr.org.
12. Quoted in Aizenman, "How to Demand a Medical Breakthrough."
13. Quoted in Terry Gross, "1st AIDS Ward '5B' Fought to Give Patients Compassionate Care, Dignified Deaths," NPR, June 26, 2019. www.npr.org.
14. Quoted in Gross, "1st AIDS Ward '5B' Fought to Give Patients Compassionate Care, Dignified Deaths."
15. Quoted in Hannah Harris Green, "Talk to Her," Slate, June 21, 2019. www.slate.com.
16. Quoted in Lillian Faderman, *The Gay Revolution: The Story of the Struggle*. New York: Simon & Schuster, 2015, p. 422.
17. Quoted in Zachary Zane, "How the Real-Life Rock Hudson from *Hollywood* Changed the AIDS Movement," *Men's Health*, May 1, 2020. www.menshealth.com.
18. David France, "The Activists," *New York Times*, April 13, 2020. www.nytimes.com.
19. Quoted in Aizenman, "How to Demand a Medical Breakthrough."

Chapter Three: The AIDS Crisis in Africa

20. Quoted in B:M 2020, "The History of AIDS in Africa." www.blackhistorymonth.org.uk/article/section/real-stories/the-history-of-aids-in-africa.
21. Nuala McGovern, "Outposts: Slim Disease," WNYC, May 8, 2008. www.wnyc.org.
22. Max Fisher, "The Story of AIDS in Africa," *The Atlantic*, December 1, 2011. www.theatlantic.com.
23. Quoted in *New York Times*, "Zambian, in Appeal, Says Son Died of AIDS," October 5, 1987. www.nytimes.com.
24. Quoted in Rory Carroll, "Former South African President's Last Son Dies of AIDS," *The Guardian* (Manchester, UK), January 6, 2005. www.theguardian.com.
25. Quoted in Sarah Boseley, "Mbeki Aids Denial 'Caused 300,000 Deaths,'" *The Guardian* (Manchester, UK), November 26, 2008. www.theguardian.com.

26. Quoted in South African History Online, "The Birth of the Treatment Action Campaign," September 30, 2019. www.sahistory.org.za.
27. Quoted in Helen Epstein, "The Fidelity Fix," *New York Times*, June 13, 2004. www.nytimes.com.

Chapter Four: Living with HIV/AIDS Today
28. Quoted in Michael Byrne, "A Brief History of AZT, HIV's First 'Ray of Hope,'" *Vice*, March 21, 2015. www.vice.com.
29. Quoted in Simon Garfield, "The Rise and Fall of AZT: It Was the Drug That Had to Work," *The Independent* (London), May 2, 1993. www.independent.co.uk.
30. Quoted in Clare Sansom, "Molecules Made to Measure," *Chemistry World*, November 2009. www.rsc.org.
31. Quoted in Mark Harrington, "Razing the House of Cards: The Discovery of HAART and the Push for Evidence-Based HIV Treatment," TheBodyPro, May 1, 2013. www.thebodypro.com.
32. Quoted in Barbara Pinto, "A Day in the Life: Living with HIV," ABC News, September 20, 2011. www.abcnews.go.com.
33. Quoted in John Paul Brammer, "Three Decades Later, Men Who Survived the 'Gay Plague' Speak Out," NBC News, December 1, 2017. www.nbcnews.com.
34. Quoted in Maggie L. Shaw, "Birx: There Have Been Gains, and Setbacks, in Our Global Fight Against HIV," *American Journal of Managed Care*, July 9, 2020. www.ajmc.com.

Books

Ruth Coker Burks, *All the Young Men: A Memoir of Love, AIDS, and Chosen Family in the American South*. New York: Grove, 2020.

Kim Yi Dionne, *Doomed Interventions: The Failure of Global Responses to AIDS in Africa*. New York: Cambridge University Press, 2017.

Ann Richardson, *Wise Before Their Time: People with AIDS and HIV Talk About Their Lives*. New York: Glenmore, 2017.

Randy Shilts, *And the Band Played On: Politics, People, and the AIDS Epidemic*. New York: St. Martin's, 2007.

Celeste Watkins-Hayes, *Remaking a Life: How Women Living with HIV/AIDS Confront Inequality*. Berkeley: University of California Press, 2019.

Internet Sources

Brian P. Dunleavy, "Fauci Sees Similarities Between HIV, COVID-19 in Public Health Response," UPI, October 16, 2020. www.upi.com.

David France, "The Activists: How ACT UP Remade Political Organizing in America," *New York Times*, April 13, 2020. www.nytimes.com.

Howard Markel, "How the Discovery of HIV Led to a Transatlantic Research War," PBS, March 24, 2020. www.pbs.org.

Esther Nakkazi, "As Uganda Takes Control of the HIV Epidemic, U.S. Shifts Funding," Undark, October 6, 2020. https://undark.org.

Emma Russell, "Aging, Overlooked, and HIV-Positive," *Vice*, December 6, 2018. www.vice.com.

Websites

Centers for Disease Control and Prevention (CDC) (www.cdc.gov). The CDC works around the clock to protect America from health, safety, and security threats, both foreign and in the United States. The CDC website contains a frequently updated section on HIV/AIDS, including a fact sheet, articles on treatment and care, and news about current research.

GMHC (www.gmhc.org). The GMHC, formerly called the Gay Men's Health Crisis, is the world's first HIV/AIDS service organization. Its mission is to end the AIDS epidemic and uplift the lives of all people affected by the disease. The GMHC website details its various programs, including assistance for HIV/AIDS patients who are experiencing problems with food and housing insecurity, unemployment, and lack of access to health services.

Joint United Nations Programme on HIV/AIDS (UNAIDS) (www.unaids.org). Founded in 1996 as a United Nations initiative, UNAIDS seeks to end the AIDS epidemic as a public health threat by 2030. The UNAIDS website explains the group's mission, provides facts about HIV/AIDS and treatments, and describes its work in many different regions of the world.

POZ (www.poz.com). POZ is an award-winning print and online brand for people living with and affected by HIV/AIDS. The website offers daily news, treatment updates, personal profiles, and investigative features on AIDS-related issues. It also features a community forum for discussion of HIV/AIDS-related issues.

INDEX

PICTURE CREDITS